CHARMING
daphne
TRUE PLATINUM SERIES

MORGANA BEVAN

CHARMING
daphne

TRUE PLATINUM SERIES

MORGANA BEVAN

*E*yes widened when I blew into the lobby of True Platinum International. I mean, I couldn't blame them. A soaking wet woman wasn't your typical sight in the swanky, marble-and glass-covered space at any time of the day, let alone 8 AM.

It probably didn't help that I limped past reception, cursing out London cabbies and my new heels.

I raced into the mercifully empty women's bathroom and started digging through the cabinets. There had to be a hairdryer in there somewhere. There was one on the twentieth floor where I worked.

If I set foot in my office looking like

a bedraggled mess, right before I had to chew out Casey Jackson for his latest stunt, I'd never live it down.

Who the hell thought it would be a good idea to go on a rampage at an award show with thirty-eight cameras available to capture every tiny detail, and livestream it to millions of watching fans?

"Casey fucking Jackson," I growled beneath my breath.

Friday mornings were supposed to be sedate. I'd dealt with enough fires in the last week. I didn't need an extra surprise right before the weekend.

"Inconsiderate rock stars."

My hand snagged on a black device buried behind a week's worth of loo roll. Packages scattered as I hissed, "Yes," and grabbed it before scooting out of the cupboard with care.

Definitely didn't need to add a concussion to today's shitshow.

No, I needed to get my hair dry and my skirt back into some semblance of appropriate for the walk across the busy lobby. Totally doable. Then I looked in the mirror.

Well, shit.

Maybe keeping my hair to my waist had been a bad move. The lot of it hung in drenched strings around my face. My makeup ran down my face. Not quite the look I wanted, even if panda circles did set my icy blue eyes off really well.

I glanced at the time on my phone. "Fuck."

Ten minutes. Ten minutes until I had to put an idiot know-it-all musician in his place.

The elevator would eat at least five of those while it stopped at every single floor.

"Shit."

I pulled a wad of paper towel from the dispenser, turned on the tap, and frantically scrubbed my face. All the while, my gaze stayed fixed on the clock.

A minute down, and my heart was racing far too flipping fast to be healthy.

I dropped the crumpled-up, blackened tissues into the bin, chewing my lip while I tried to sort through the best course of action.

No point wasting time drying my suit. I kept a change of clothes in my office. I just had to face the mortification of the looks I'd get in the lift.

My face could stay bare, too. My boss might not like it so much, but needs must.

Four minutes.

I scooped up the hairdryer and rammed the plug into the socket, then I nuked my hair with the highest heat setting. The door opened while I bent over with my hair flung over to one side creating a curtain around me, muttering a string of curses.

"Are you alright?" a strong Scottish voice asked.

I straightened fast, directing a perfectly sane smile at her. She looked barely twenty-five, and if I didn't look too closely, she could have been my sister.

Only I didn't have one.

So really, letting her vaguely familiar features slow me down would be a stupid idea…

"Fine. A cab got me." I shrugged before turning my back on her.

I tracked her in the mirror while directing the hairdryer back to the unruly mop of hair.

She frowned but said no more before disappearing into a stall. I'd been so fresh and optimistic when I was her age. Newly passed the bar and the perfect job lined up. An amazing boyfriend who also worked at the record label. We could have commuted together and shared our woes on hard days with very little explanation.

I have no idea why I romanticised it like that. It would have just been work… but I'd wanted things to fall into place so badly.

Until he sabotaged my chance of getting that job.

Pressure prickled behind my eyes and I glared at my reflection.

What the hell do you think you're doing, going there?

I'd promised myself five years ago that I'd stop torturing myself with what might have been. I'd meant it then and I meant it now. Traitorous Matt Brodie had no place in my thoughts.

With my hair mostly dry and the clock screaming that I had less than two minutes, I swept my hair into as clean a bun as I could manage.

Handbag in one hand and phone in the other, I rushed out of the bathroom, my painful heels clattering against the hard floor while my fingers flew over the keys, texting my work wife.

Daphne: SOS. Got caught in the rain. Can you pull out my spare suit for me?

Dots danced in the chat box and I willed it to move faster.

A message pinged on the screen just as I barrelled into a hard surface. My heels slipped out from beneath me and I tipped backwards. My phone slipped from my fingers, clattering to the ground. Probably cracked the screen.

For fucks sake, give a girl a break.

Arms wrapped around me, strong fingers dug into my sides stopping my downward trajectory.

"Sorry, lass. I wasn't looking. Are you alright?"

My heart stopped as that voice swept over me.

With great hesitation, I lifted my head. My stomach churned with the certainty of what waited for me.

What the hell did I do to deserve this level of shit in one morning?

Matt's familiar green gaze stared back at me with concern. Five years had aged him well. A scruff of a ginger beard covered his jaw, somehow making him hotter. How the hell was that fair?

His concern quickly morphed into something I couldn't read. He righted me and I stepped away from him so fast you'd think he'd burned me.

"Matt," I spat.

He rubbed his neck. Despite his rugged professional vibes, in a suit that hugged him a little too well for my imagination, old habits died hard. He'd held on to his tells, and I made him uncomfortable.

Too right he should be uncomfortable. Rat bastard had used his sway to keep me out of a job.

"It's been ages, Daphne." The way that brogue licked at my name almost sent a shiver down my spine. Almost. He knelt and picked up my phone. "I didn't know you were working in the building."

My eyes narrowed on him as he straightened. "Why did you need to know? You can't get me fired from this one."

I took the phone and brushed past him, striding towards the bank of elevators with determination. And maybe a slightly too aggressive swing of my hips.

I'm well within my rights to torture the ass.

A quick glance at my phone didn't settle my nerves. My heart raced, the pressure centred in my throat, making it incredibly difficult to breathe or think.

Ivy had my suit, and Casey hadn't arrived yet, so I had time. That should have relieved me.

Yet if I held my hand still, it shook. *Fucking Matt Brodie.*

I'd worked in the building for six months, handling the legal damage control for the biggest of True Platinum's artists. Of course, I'd known Rhiannon were signed to Pryderi Records, which TPI owned, but that didn't mean I had to see Matt. Band managers didn't spend their lives in this place.

Why was he even here?

I stopped in front of the elevators. A crowd of people gathered, eyes fixed on their phones, feet tapping impatiently while the lifts took their sweet time arriving.

A throat cleared next to me, and my eyes fell shut on a desperate plea for control. I couldn't start shouting at my ex in front of the staff. He knew better. We'd closed this lid. He wouldn't…

"Could we catch up later, Daph?"

"Not a chance," I muttered, trying to keep my voice low.

I may as well have shouted it. Heads came up, and backs tensed in front of me. Every damn person in my vicinity was listening intently. Fuck.

I shot Matt a look filled with murderous warning. He just stared back at me with confusion.

The lift pinged its arrival and the doors opened. People in front of me filed on, and I edged forward, willing there to not be enough space for us both.

No such luck, of course. I don't know why I expected anything more. The universe had decided to dump on me.

With my stomach sinking to the marble ground, I stepped into the car. The doors shut, and no matter how I moved, my shoulder brushed against Matt's. Such an innocent, inconsequential touch should not have had my smutty mind racing into the gutter, but try talking sense after a morning of stress.

Matt tilted his head towards me and I held my breath, waiting for the sod to try and reason with me in a very public space.

"So how've you been?" Matt asked.

Every inch of my body stiffened. "You don't need to talk to me."

Matt chuckled. "Okay, but I want to."

"Then stop the wanting, and shut up."

By the time the nightmare ended, everyone in the building would think of me as a colossal bitch. And I would own it.

They didn't know what this man had taken from me. They could judge all they wanted but Matt Brodie was dead to me.

The lift stopped on the third floor and a swarm of people cleared out. It barely dented the headcount inside the metal box. My neck itched with the pressure of their gazes, and I bit the inside of my cheek hard to stop myself from shouting at them.

Do not drag innocent people into your nightmare, Daphne.

"When did you start working here?"

I sighed as I turned my head to glare at him. "Seriously? I tell you to shut up and you go with that?"

He smirked. "Just curious, Nymphy."

Why did one word have the power to cut me off at the knees? Surely that shouldn't be possible. Yet the sound of that stupid pet name rolling off his tongue, wrapped up in that delicious accent, still made me weak in the knees.

"Stop calling me that. Stop talking. Stop looking at me." I breathed in deep, trying to control the spiralling pressure behind the words. "Just stop."

Matt's brows rose, something a little too close to amusement shining at me in those deep green eyes. If he kept looking at me like that, I might murder him with my shoe.

The door opened again on the fifth floor, ridding me of a couple more witnesses.

Half a dozen suits remained, all of them now looking vaguely uncomfortable. Good. That's what you got for eavesdropping on private, annoying and unwanted conversations.

"Thought we agreed to stay friends?"

"Fucking hell. You can't quit can you?"

Matt turned toward me, giving up all semblance of relaxation and disinterest. "I'm highly confused, so no I'm not going to quit."

I faced off with him too. Avoidance be damned. If he wanted to keep pushing, I'd give him what he wanted.

"If you wanted a friend, Matt, you shouldn't have sabotaged me to protect your fucking ego." My voice might have risen with each word.

The doors opened again on the eighth floor, and another two suits disembarked, shooting us odd looks over their shoulders. Oh yes, there would definitely be a company-wide memo going around before I got to my desk.

"You were obsessed with us working together, Daphne. And I was leaving the label." He held his hands out at his sides in that universal sign of frustration. "I don't understand you right now."

"Oh yes, for your precious band. I remember." I crossed my arms. "Hear that worked out well for you. Your new girl good with you never being home?"

His eyes narrowed on me and his jaw ticked. "I forgot how frustrating you could be." He dragged a hand through his hair before turning away from me.

"So that's a no then? Too bad."

"Like you're doing any better," he muttered. Unfortunately, his words still carried over the annoying elevator music.

For a music company, you'd think they'd pump in some decent music. Probably too cheap to pay their own royalty fees.

"I am, thanks." It was a total lie but he didn't need to know that.

He spun around, smirking at me with far too much knowledge.

"Oh yeah? What's his name?"

A name. I could pull absolutely any random name. It didn't need to sound believable. He'd never bloody know it was a lie.

Yet nothing came and my tongue fused itself to the roof of my mouth.

"Thought so." He shook his head and turned back to the door.

The lift stopped on the tenth floor and I glared at the counter. Could it not just make a run for the twentieth and free me? Why was that too much to ask of fate after all it had dealt me already today?

The remaining suits rushed out. With just the two of us left, the doors shut,' and we separated to our own corners. I frowned at the control panel, at the singular light highlighting our next floor. Why was he going to the twentieth?

"I didn't sabotage you, Nymphy."

"Stop calling me that," I growled. I refused to look at him.

His calm demeanour chafed against my expectations. How could he be so unaffected by his own bullshit? I needed to get my emotions under control. I couldn't keep ceding so much power to him.

"Okay," he gritted out. "But I didn't sabotage you."

"Really? What would you call it when someone gets offered a job and then it miraculously goes away after she tells you about it?"

Matt dragged a hand across his face.

"'Cause I'd definitely call that sabotage, but what would I know? I clearly wasn't a great judge of character." I glared at him, all of that old hurt roaring to the surface. "You were so weird about it, too."

I hadn't thought I'd bottled it up. My friends had heard my woes on repeat back then, to the point that they got sick of hearing me repeat it. But with the amount of vehemence coating my words, I must have done.

And that pissed me off even more.

"Now c'mon, Daphne. You can't write off everything we had over one thing." He pushed off the elevator wall, his body tense beneath that slate grey suit.

I couldn't stop my gaze from tracking down his torso. Couldn't stop my mind from throwing up far too many images of his naked body, sprawled out in my bed.

"Watch me," I muttered under my breath.

"Watch me?" Matt's brows climbed. "When did you start acting like a toddler?"

My mouth dropped open and Matt's eyes fell shut on a groan.

"Shit. I didn't mean that."

"No, I think you did. What else did you keep to yourself, Mattie?" I stepped towards him before sense could take control of my movements. "Maybe some idiotic belief that I wasn't good enough for your record label?"

Matt surged towards me, denial written across his earnest face. It couldn't be earnest. If it was, he never would have talked me out of a job. My instincts about this man had been wrong. I needed to accept that and if I couldn't do it five years ago, now would be a good time to start.

The lift jolted hard, and the lights flickered. I lost my footing and almost fell into the doors. Strong hands caught me around the waist. Matt pulled me into his chest before bracing himself against the wall.

For the second time today, Matt Brodie saved me from a painful fall. Indignation flooded me, and I opened my mouth to demand he let me go.

Then the lift jolted again, bucking hard enough for my feet to leave the floor and ripping a scream from my throat. The blood drained from my face as the lights went out.

We couldn't be trapped. It had to be a fluke.

I tried to relax, tried to will myself from Matt's arms, but every inch of me locked up with fear. I'd never been trapped in an elevator, had no idea what we were meant to do.

Could we plummet to our deaths?

"Breathe, Nymphy." Matt squeezed me, reminding me that he still held me. "It'll be alright."

Easy for him to say. He wasn't trapped with the person who'd broken his heart.

CHAPTER TWO

*M*att pressed the call button on the control panel a couple of times. With each attempt, the pressure in my chest tightened.

We were seriously trapped.

For all of a minute, I'd managed to convince myself that it was a drill. They were just testing us.

But the longer the silence filled the car, the more serious our situation became.

"It'll be okay, Daphne." He turned back to me, giving up on the call button entirely. "They'll get us out of here. We just have to stay calm and be patient."

I stared at him, shock slackening my jaw. He couldn't be serious. Stay calm? In a metal box that could hurtle us to our deaths without warning?

"We aren't going to hurtle to our deaths. There are safety mechanisms to stop that."

My eyes widened as he answered the unspoken question.

"You're an open book, Nymphy."

"Stop. Calling. Me. That," I ground out.

He nodded but said nothing more as he returned to pressing the call button.

I pulled my phone from my handbag. Ivy would get me out of here.

No signal.

Heart on the floor, I held the device up in the air, hunting fruitlessly for a signal.

Fuck.

Not only was I trapped with my ex, but I would also almost certainly be late for a very important meeting.

I knew I shouldn't have gotten in the lift with Matt. Seeing him this morning had been unfortunate enough. He was a bad bloody omen.

No, I had to get out of here. I couldn't lose another job because of him.

I dropped the phone into my purse and began searching for a way out. I scrambled towards the door. Digging my fingers into the seam holding the door shut, I tried to pull them apart.

It looked so easy on TV, but in reality, they didn't so much as budge. And my efforts were rewarded with a broken nail.

"What are you doing, Daphne?"

I couldn't focus on Matt, couldn't stand still really.

"Trying to find a way out."

My gaze scanned the tiny space, searching for options. Anything to help me escape Matt and prevent the latest destruction of my hard work.

The trap door in the ceiling.

I rushed towards it with the briefest flutter of excitement in my belly.

That excitement died when I stood

beneath it and realised that I couldn't reach it. I turned to Matt, studying him as I chewed my lip. Maybe if he…

Matt stared back at me with his brows raised and his arms crossed. "I am not lifting you up there."

"Why the hell not?" I stamped my foot like the toddler he accused me of being earlier.

"What are you going to do? Scale the elevator shaft in a pair of designer heels and a mini-skirt?"

"This is not a mini-skirt," I growled, focusing on the wrong thing.

"It will be by the time you get up there."

"Fine, don't help me."

I turned my back on him, kicking off my shoes. If I could get up on the rail surrounding the lift, I might be able to reach the trap door.

With a barely formed plan, I gripped the rail and flung a foot up on the opposite bar. Then I froze. How the hell was I meant to get up without falling back on my head?

Matt's arms wrapped around my waist, pulling me back away from the railing.

"Are you trying to get yourself killed? Just stop," he muttered, his breath shaky against my neck. "Please just stop."

I shook off his grip, bursting from his arms and spinning to face him. A distant part of me recognised that I wasn't acting rationally, but it couldn't compete with the fear.

"I'm not going to sit down and wait to die while you moan about how much better I could be." A spark of anger lit inside of me and I grabbed it with both hands. Anything but the terror bubbling up, trying to steal my voice.

"I would never say something like that to you," he said, his voice and his expression calm. Or as calm as one could be in our situation. "You were incredible, Daphne. I highly doubt that's changed in five years."

I snorted. "That why you robbed me of an opportunity?"

He sighed.

"You know you could have just told me you didn't want to work with me?" I shrugged, pretending those words didn't hurt still. "I never would have applied if I'd known you hated the idea that much."

"I didn't hate the idea. I just…"

"You just what?" I stepped toward him, my gaze riveted by the warring emotions on his handsome face.

His shoulders sagged. "We were starting something new. It was important, and working together would have ruined it." His gaze roamed my face, searching for something, but hell if I knew what.

"So you should have said that. Instead, you turned into a crazy cryptic man."

"Hardly." He crossed his arms again.

"Oh? So trying to figure out if I knew people who worked at Cleo Records wasn't you being cryptic?"

"Of course not, I was curious."

I snorted. "I've seen you curious, Matt. It looks a lot different."

Curious for Matt equalled sly smiles and focused attention. Instead, he'd given me frowns and sideways glances.

"We might have only been together for four months, but I knew you." My hands landed on my hips while I scowled at him. "You couldn't fool me that easily then, and you definitely can't now."

If I could never lay eyes on him again, I'd be a happy woman. My focus returned to the task of getting free.

"You actually think it would have been easy to work together?" Incredulity filled his voice. I didn't turn around. He could talk to my bun. "You haven't seen me when I'm stressed, Nymphy. It's not pleasant."

"Well, it doesn't matter now." I frowned up at the door. *Maybe if I jumped?* "And for the last time, stop calling me that."

"If you stop thinking about getting up there, I will."

"We aren't bargaining here." I glanced at him over my shoulder, glaring hard. "You lost the right to call me sweet things when you took control of my career without my permission."

"What the hell do you want from me, Daphne? We're stuck here, I can't fix that. And I did what I thought was best for us back then, I also can't change that."

I froze at his words. Slowly, I turned on my stocking-covered heel, my mind running circles around those simple words.

He dragged a hand down his face and turned his back on me, completely obvious to the cogs turning in my head.

"Did you just..." I frowned, chewing over his meaning again. "Did you just admit to getting in the way of my job offer?"

He spun back around, his eyes narrowed. "I said no such thing."

"Yes, you did." I took a large step

forward, stopping only when my finger pressed against his chest. "You did what was best for us? What the hell was best for us, Matt? Me not working at your bloody label?"

He shook his head.

"Do not lie to me right now. You already let the words slip." I jabbed at his chest, punctuating each point. "For once in your bloody life, tell me the truth."

He leaned back, his gaze focused on the ceiling while he released a measured breath. My guard went up immediately.

"Fine," he growled before fixing those mesmerising green eyes on me. "It would have been a conflict of interest."

"What?" I spluttered.

"What if one of my bands screwed up, and we disagreed over the solution?" His brows rose in question when all I could do was open and close my mouth. Shock stole my voice. "You would have had to act in Cleo Records' best interest and I would have been acting for the band."

"We would have —" I shook my head, struggling to form a coherent argument.

"What? Talked it out? Come to a compromise?"

I jerked my chin in agreement.

"What if the label's best solution was to cut the band, and I asked you to advise differently?"

"You wouldn't have." I swallowed hard, not really believing myself.

"Would you be willing to stake your career on it?" His voice deepened, the words barely more than a rumble. Despite the severity of the question they still managed to send a spark of interest to my nerve endings.

I chewed my lip instead of answering, and he nodded, his lips tipping up in a sardonic smile.

"Didn't think so." He stepped away from me and my hand dropped back to my side, leaving me feeling oddly brevet.

"Then it's a good thing we split

up," I muttered, cursing myself as the horrid sounds left my mouth. "I could never trust a man with no integrity."

He laughed, the sound mirthless. "Should have known you'd take it that way."

"How else was I meant to take you putting business before me?" I muttered, turning back to the emergency hatch.

Matt growled behind me. "Will you stop with that fucking trap door?"

He gripped my arm, spinning me around. I tipped my head back, staring into his face while he backed me to the elevator wall.

"I'm not going to let you hurt yourself, so stop thinking about it."

My brows rose. "Seriously? You're worked up about me getting hurt now?" I rose up on my tiptoes. "Maybe you should have thought of that before you screwed me over."

"For the last time," he bit out, leaning closer until our noses almost touched. "I didn't screw you over."

I opened my mouth, a retort on the

tip of my tongue to reduce him to dust. He slammed his lips against mine before I could utter a single word. His tongue thrust into my mouth, claiming me and swallowing my startled groan.

For a second, I just stood there while he kissed me, while his grip on my arm loosened and his hands fell to my hips.

There's a reason you should stop this…

The feel of those firm hands taking control of my body did me in.

My fingers glided up his torso and I leaned into him, leaned into the bruising caress of his lips against mine. I gripped his hair, urging him closer while he tugged me forward, fitting me perfectly against his body.

We were wild, punishing yet pleasuring each other with our bodies. A throb started in my core, begging me to get closer.

I whimpered when his lips left mine. It very quickly turned to moans as he trailed open-[mouth kisses across my jaw and down my neck. He sucked at the skin between my shoulder and neck, sending heated shivers down my spine.

My nipples hardened painfully against my damp bra.

More. Gimme more.

I tugged at his shirt, ripping it from his grey suit trousers. He grinned against my skin then he lifted his head and claimed my lips again. His hand dove into my hair, undoing my bun with very little effort. My hair fell, and he used it to his advantage, tilting his head and deepening our connection.

His other hand trailed from my waist down my thigh, to the edge of my skirt. The tips of his fingers grazed my leg, and the muscles clenched tight while heat licked my skin. He dragged the material up, up and up. Then he gripped my leg and lifted it, leaning into me.

My breath whooshed out at the satisfying press of his hardness against me. Matt held my leg high against his hip. He leaned back, watching my expression with hooded lids, while he rocked against me. My eyes just about rolled back at the first flutter of pleasure. He'd positioned himself perfectly to grind against my clit and with each rock, my ability to stay upright crumbled.

Matt wrapped his other arm around my waist and held me to him. He claimed my lips again, devouring every moan that escaped me.

I shouldn't be doing this.

But it felt so good.

Pressure started to build inside of me and my eyelids grew heavier. Fuck, he was really going to make me orgasm in an elevator.

It should feel wrong. Yet it just made my need soar.

I ground against him, taking everything he was willing to give. His kisses slowed while he worked me towards the edge. It almost felt too personal, too soft.

I wanted the hard, passionate rush back. It felt safer.

My eyes fell shut as the orgasm finally tore through me. I sagged against him. My cheeks heated but I lacked the energy to push him away.

"You guys alright in there?" A male voice asked, invading the silence cocooning us.

My eyes flew open and Matt's body stiffened against me. He released my leg before stepping back. He slowly released me, studying me but not really meeting my gaze.

When I didn't collapse into a heap at his feet, he turned towards the control panel and the phone there.

"We're okay for the minute," Matt said into the phone, his voice surprisingly steady considering the size of the bulge in his trousers. "How long are we going to be stuck?"

"I'm not sure, man. It could be a couple of hours. I'll try to keep you updated but the maintenance crew are about an hour away so sit tight for now."

What else were we meant to do?

My gaze rose to the hatch above my head again.

"We'll do that," Matt muttered, his voice hard.

When I looked up, I found him glaring at me. Despite our history, despite the fact I should hate him, did hate him, I blushed.

att closed the door on the phone without breaking eye contact. The glow of the orgasm faded quickly but the need for more still thumbed through me.

And that pissed me off more than him glaring at me.

"Don't do that again."

His brows rose. "Don't do what, exactly? Stop your stupid plans to escape or give you an orgasm?"

"Both."

"You used to be reasonable after I made you come." He sighed.

"You used to not be an ass. We can't all win."

His lips quirked in a smile but it

didn't reach his eyes. In fact, he looked sad. My heart twinged as regret flickered in my mind, but that just wouldn't do.

I squashed it before it could fester and make me question my every choice with him. He'd made his bed, he could deal with the fallout.

The floor really didn't look comfortable, but if we were going to be trapped for hours, I might as well sit. I settled in the opposite corner to him, leaning back against the wall and drawing my knees up.

At least my clothes had almost dried.

It wasn't lost on me that, had I not dried my hair, I wouldn't have gotten trapped in the elevator or run into him.

"Fucking fate."

"What was that?" Matt asked. His brow furrowed.

"Nothing," I muttered. "Nothing at all."

He settled on the floor near me with a quiet grumble. I couldn't catch the words, and I didn't have the energy to care.

"Could you not sit on that side of the lift?" I pointed toward the control panel opposite me.

Matt didn't answer. He leaned his head against the wall and shut his eyes.

"That's the complete opposite of what I asked."

"Nymphy, we're going to be stuck here for a while, can we please just be civil?" He kept his voice low but I didn't miss the satisfied curling of his lips at the thought of us being civil.

What we'd just done suggested we were more than civil. It suggested I'd forgiven him.

Which I hadn't.

Because none of it made sense…

My mind whirled, throwing memory after memory at me. Something didn't sit right about his story, but I couldn't put my finger on it.

"What aren't you telling me?" I muttered to myself, my eyes closed.

"What?"

I ignored him.

A reel of our short time together played through my mind. Both the happy moments and our explosive end. He'd barely fought me when I accused him of getting between me and the job back then. He'd just rolled over and taken it. Which, thinking about it now, made no sense.

For the majority of our time together, we'd been amazing. He'd been so thoughtful, helping me study for my exams and listening patiently while I worked my way through a difficult case. He'd kept me fuelled but distracted me when I needed a break and didn't realise it. He'd always seemed to know I was near my breaking point before I did.

I almost let that realisation deter me from finding the thing making me uneasy.

He contradicted himself.

"Either you're lying to me now, or you lied to me then," I whispered to myself.

I glanced at Matt with such sharpness that his eyes clouded with concern.

"What is it?" He sat forward. "Are you okay?"

"Why did you tell me we'd make an awesome duo in the music world, if you thought it would be a conflict of interest?"

Slowly, he sank back against the wall. All the colour drained from his face, and I knew, I just knew I'd caught him in a lie.

"Which was it, Matt?" My voice hardened, the conviction of my beliefs fuelling me.

He rubbed his forehead. His eyes shut but his entire body tensed.

"You lied about the job, didn't you?"

I shifted forward onto my knees, edging towards him like a moth to a flame. Staying put, keeping distance between us would have been the sensible thing to do but I couldn't. I needed answers and Matt had never liked the pressure of someone getting in his face.

He opened his eyes and fixed me with a pleading look. I had no intention of easing up. So instead, I moved closer.

"If our relationship meant anything to you, Matt, you'll tell me the truth."

He shook his head, regret darkening his eyes. "I wish I could, but I signed an NDA."

I sat back on my haunches. Shock rippled through me. That I'd got an answer. That he'd admitted to hiding something from me. But was it an admission that he'd ruined my chances at the job on purpose?

My head tilted to the side as I considered him.

"That's why you asked me all those weird questions," I whispered, the pieces finally falling into place.

He nodded but pressed his lips together.

"What did all those names have to do with your NDA?"

Matt groaned. "If I could have told

you that, I would have done it five years ago and saved us. I can't."

Pressure built behind my eyes while his expression begged me to let it go.

"So you did throw us away for your job?" Somehow my voice didn't break like my heart did.

Why did I let him have that power over me after all these years?

"No, Daphne, I—"

"Stop lying to me, Matt," I snapped. "What did the NDA have to do with the job?"

Again he shook his head.

Pressure built in my throat, the need to scream in frustration unbearable. I never did that. I was the articulate, calm one. My words solved problems. But he made me want to tear something apart with my bare hands.

Instead, I forced myself to take a deep breath. Releasing it, I willed the frustration to go with it. I couldn't figure him out if anger clouded my mind.

"The NDA wasn't about hiring practices?"

He pressed his lips together and glanced away. His shoulders dropped while he focused on the doors, anything to not look at me. *Well, tough shit, Mattie, all you've got is me.*

I shifted position until I kneeled in front of him, so close I blocked his view of anything else. So close I might as well have been straddling him.

"I'm not going to let it go." I leaned forward, placing my hands on the wall. "We don't know how long we're going to be in here and you know I can be annoying when I need to be. So spill."

"I wanted to tell you then, Daph, but it would have hurt Rhiannon. The band was too new to deal with the kind of fallout it would have caused." He begged me to let it go. Those green eyes bore into mine.

I almost felt sorry for him and then another piece of the puzzle clicked.

"You didn't trust me," I whispered, sitting back again.

My gaze focused on the pinstripes running through his trousers. I couldn't look at his face. Bad enough my eyes were wide, mirroring the shock squirming painfully through my chest.

"I loved you, and you didn't trust me to keep my mouth shut." I glanced up at him, my lips flatlining. "We didn't really stand a chance, did we?"

"Yes, we did." He reached for me as I shuffled to back my corner, missing my arm by inches. "Daphne, listen to me."

"No. What would be the point?" I held my hand out to stop him when he tensed. "We clearly aren't going to agree. You won't tell me what could be so bad you'd let an NDA come between us, and I think you're full of shit."

"I was trying to protect you."

"All you wanted to protect was your precious band." I shook my head. "Let's stop talking. I'd really like to not stab you with my heel, Matt, but keep pissing me off and I just might."

He didn't believe me, of course. I

didn't believe me. The words lacked any kind of strength.

The man had always been able to take me to emotional highs. It was exhausting and I needed to numb myself against it, against him. We would never agree. Continuing to try only wasted my breath.

Matt settled back against his corner and let his head thump against the metal wall.

"If I ever see that piece of shit again, I'll be the one committing murder, Daphne," he muttered, his voice so low I had to strain to catch them.

I frowned at the wall in front of me. *What the hell was he talking about?*

CHAPTER FOUR

*H*alf an hour later, my stomach grumbled. I'd skipped breakfast, and in all the stress of getting drenched by a cab, seeing Matt and getting stuck in the lift, I'd forgotten I had food in my bag.

Plus, someone had cranked the bloody heat up.

Sweat beaded on my face, making me extremely glad I'd washed my makeup off. There was nothing worse than sweating with a layer of foundation blocking my pores.

Well, maybe getting trapped in an elevator with the ex who could still make you mindless with lust...

I rifled through my handbag, far

too aware of Matt following my every move. It wouldn't stop being weird, sharing air with him.

Probably didn't help that I kept replaying my stupid slip of the tongue on repeat.

Why the hell did I tell him I'd loved him?

I could have happily gone the rest of my life without him understanding just how much his actions had fucked with me. Or how much I'd trusted him.

Then I had to go and blurt it out like it was some ridiculous trump card.

At least he hadn't tried to talk about it.

Actually, the silence might have been worse. He could have at least acknowledged my slip of the tongue.

I pulled an apple and a protein bar from my handbag before I spiralled into an angry pity party. If I carried on down that path, I'd never be able to talk to him civilly.

But did I want to talk to him at all?

Blocking unnecessary distractions

was something of a speciality of mine. If I really wanted to, I could pretend he wasn't trapped with me.

I eyed him from beneath my lashes, head thrown back, eyes shut, relaxed for once. Would it be so bad if we escaped the lift without tearing each other's throats out?

"Do you want the apple or the protein bar?"

His gaze dropped to the items in my hands and back to my face. Surprise flickered in his green eyes.

"I'm not falling for that." He faced forward, crossing his arms.

"I'm serious."

"You don't share food."

"Well, I'm offering."

He was right. Ordinarily, I wouldn't. If someone so much as looked at my plate or snacks, I turned into a growling she-wolf.

"There's no fork, Matt. You're safe."

Matt grunted, the sound non-committal.

Exasperation and residual annoyance at him forced the air from my lungs. I shifted onto my knees and shuffled towards him.

"It's not a trick." I stopped when his leg bumped against mine. "Will you just pick one?"

He studied me with narrowed eyes. "I'd rather you not hold this against me."

"Don't worry, I won't." I shrugged, my smirk barely hidden. "I have plenty of other things to hold over you."

He smiled before glancing down at my offerings. "I'll take the apple."

"Are you sure? That's barely going to tide you over."

Matt laughed, the sound of it skirting along every single nerve ending in my body. Clearly, I'd waited too long to find a new hook-up partner.

"You might claim you're fine with sharing right now, but that bar is mint chocolate, and contrary to your opinions of me, I'm not stupid."

I bit my lip, trying to hold back my own laughter. Okay, so I was really bad with sharing food. He'd made his point. Even if my grip did tighten on my favourite mint chocolate chip protein bar.

"I'm good, Nymphy." He pried the apple from my grip.

We settled down and ate our snacks in silence. I wished my mind would join in on the calm. Instead, it squirrelled away at the NDA problem.

Why had he signed one? If he couldn't say it definitely didn't apply to hiring practices, was it a HR related NDA? Did it protect a specific person or the business as a whole?

Surely if it related to a specific person, he could have dropped me hints once I started. But then, why would a company have an NDA for an employee if that employee were troublesome enough to require an NDA? Logically, they would just rid themselves of the liability.

None of it made sense, but I could feel the anger fizzling out. I'm not sure I liked that development, especially not after he drove me to orgasm so easily after so many years apart. My cheeks burned just thinking about it.

What if there were cameras in the lift? Did he consider that before he kissed me? Probably not.

Knowing Matt, he'd taken that one moment of weakness as permission to brush all of our issues aside.

Issue. Singular.

NDA or not, he still put himself and his band ahead of my fledgling career without discussion.

I should have stopped him.

"Whatever you're working yourself up to, please stop."

I glared at him. "How do you know I'm thinking anything?"

"Oh, I know. I spent five months with you." He chuckled. He gestured to my face and my eyes narrowed. "Your eyes glaze over when you're lost in thought. And when it's dangerous and going to lead to an argument, you start frowning." His brows rose, challenging me to deny it. He knew I couldn't. "So whatever you're working yourself up to start, let's not."

I stared at him, my mouth dropping slightly. How had he noticed that in such a short time? Until the end, we didn't argue. We didn't have a reason to.

"I'm not that oblivious, Daphne." He smirked while I side-eyed him. "I spent a good hour studying your expression the night we first met. You ran gauntlet of emotions while your date talked incessantly."

"Stalker, much?" I rolled my eyes. "If you'd opened with that line that night, we wouldn't have had even five months."

"True." He nodded, still grinning. "But you liked me a whole lot more than your date, so I'll take the win."

I shook my head at his ridiculousness. As if he could win when we hadn't lasted.

We'd met in a restaurant in SoHo a little over five years ago. I had been on a terrible date— so terrible the guy's eye wandered to every pretty woman who walked passed while he interrupted me non-stop, then he decided he'd order for me without consulting me and chose very wrong.

Halfway out the door, Matt abandoned his dinner meeting, caught my arm and charmed me into grabbing a drink with him to blow off the burn of anger I couldn't shake.

Two weeks later, we were officially a couple, and for the first time since secondary school, I allowed myself to seriously consider what my future might look like with a man in it. Clearly, he'd made me uncharacteristically optimistic, because I didn't entertain idiotic thoughts like that.

"When did you start considering a loss a win?" I tugged at the sleeve of my suit jacket, fighting for space between it and my boiling hot arms. "I don't remember you telling stories about your negative experiences."

I noted Matt's head rolling towards me in my periphery but chose to ignore him in favour of escaping my suffocating jacket.

"You were hardly a negative story," he muttered his voice dry.

I sighed as I dropped the jacket on the floor next to me.

"We must have different memories." I shook my head. "We did a lot of shouting that last week. I threw a mug at you."

"But you missed." Amusement danced in his eyes, making me frown.

"I didn't intend to."

"I know, Nymphy." Matt chuckled.

"How can you laugh about that?" I asked, horror in my voice. I rolled up my blouse sleeves, hoping it would save me from overheating.

"I fell for you because of your feisty nature. Why would it turn me off?"

Speechless, I stared at the lift doors while my fingers plucked at the top buttons on my blouse.

I fell for you.

What!

Did he mean them like I did, that he loved me back then? Or did he mean in general when he decided to pursue me?

My mouth opened, fully intending to ask the question, and then common sense slammed into me and I pressed my lips together.

The answer wouldn't matter. It would just fill me with regrets.

"Yes, I loved you, Nymphy."

I froze.

He sighed. "If I thought I could break the NDA back then and have us all escape unscathed, I would have. But that wasn't an option."

"It might not have been an option, but you could have tried harder." I scrambled to my feet. "You could have talked to me, told me to avoid the company before I applied, told me you were planning to leave. Anything would have been better than letting me fall in love with the idea of it all and then ripping it away from me."

"I know, I didn't handle it well." Matt stood, holding his hands out in an attempt to placate me.

"Oh don't downplay it. If you wanted a job offer rescinded, bad-mouthing the candidate to the head of the company is the perfect way to go," I muttered, shooting him a droll look.

When they'd called to take back the offer, they'd mentioned personal references from highly esteemed colleagues, and I'd known.

Every inch of my body broke out in a fine sweat. I tugged my blouse out of my skirt and started flapping it, creating the tinniest breeze.

"I'm sorry, Daphne. I should have handled it better."

His gaze roamed my face, jolting between my expression and the incessant movement of my arms. He frowned.

"Are you okay?"

I turned away from him, studying the ceiling intently, hunting for a fan. "Does it feel like they turned up the heat, or am I imagining it?"

I knew I wasn't. His face was red and shiny. The only difference between us was his still enacted clothing.

"It's definitely getting hotter." He loosened his tie, but his focus remained zeroed in on me. "We've done this dance long enough, Daph. I've spent five years without you. Is there ever a chance you'll forgive me?"

"How can you think straight in this heat?" I shrugged my blouse off one shoulder, fully intent on taking it off.

Matt jolted forward, pinched the edges of my blouse, holding it shut.

"What the hell are you doing?" His jaw hardened. "Are you testing me?"

I frowned, hot air robbing me of my ability to think straight. "What are you talking about?"

"You're pissed at me. I don't need you to add me letting you strip off in an elevator to the mix."

He tugged the shirt, trying to hold the edges closed without touching me, but he overshot and knocked me off balance. I fell into him for the third time in a matter of hours. He released my shirt, grasping my hips before I could fall.

His green gaze captured all of my attention. Something squeezed in my chest the longer I stared into his eyes. It wasn't need, although he'd certainly never looked better, firm muscle lay beneath my hands, and I knew his kisses were as intoxicating as I'd remembered.

No, something about this moment softened me. Hell if I knew what it was. A tiny voice whispered that I should probably question it, but I didn't want to. I'd missed the warmth and security being in his arms had always gifted me.

Before the job debacle, he'd always been caring and considerate, which explained why the revelation had blindsided me at the time. He'd taken a next-level interest in my life that no one else ever had. He'd been eager to meet my parents, desperate for our first holiday together, constantly presenting me with little gifts at the perfect moment, usually when my studies started to stress me out.

I had the job I'd wanted desperately back then. The whole ordeal hadn't stopped me getting into the music business as legal consul like I'd feared it would. I was happy.

Mostly.

I'd be lying to myself if I continued to ignore the hole he'd left inside of me.

"What's going through that devious mind of yours?" Matt asked as he scanned my face with narrowed eyes. "There are cogs turning, but I can't tell if they're good or bad for me."

"My mind is hardly devious."

He hummed, committing to silence.

"If five years ago happened again, what would you do differently?"

Matt pursed his lips as he eyed me. "Are you being serious, or is this another trick to start an argument?"

"Entirely serious."

He didn't look convinced.

"Honestly. I want to know the answer."

I *needed* to know.

"I would have stopped you before you applied." He paused, searching my face for clues. I nodded, and he continued, "if that didn't work, I'd have at least told you I was leaving to lessen the appeal of it."

I smiled and he tilted his head.

"So you are testing me?"

I rolled my eyes. "It's hardly a test. I want to know if you've learnt anything in the last five years."

"Maybe not, but the answer is definitely yes." His grip tightened on my hip. "Now, I'd talk to you before doing something that affected us or you. Then, I was arrogant and I tried to protect you without taking your wants into account. I'll *never* make that mistake again."

Good answer, but everyone thought they'd act differently in theory.

"You don't believe me?" His brows rose in disbelief.

"I believe you *think* you'd talk to me first." I shrugged. "Only time will tell if that's true."

A small smile tugged at his lips. "Is this your way of giving me a second chance?"

Was it? I chewed my lip, considering it.

I couldn't deny that I craved this feeling. The warmth of his touch and the softness in his green eyes relaxed something inside of me. Did I really want to deny myself that for another five years?

"What if I am?"

His face lit up and his arms wrapped around me, hugging me tight to his chest. "Then I'll do everything in my power to make sure I never spend five years without you again."

CHAPTER FIVE

*M*att pulled back, smiling wider than I'd ever seen. "When we get out of here, I'm taking you to lunch. I'll order champagne and we'll mark the occasion properly."

I smiled at the thought even though I couldn't escape logic. "I'd love to, but I'll probably have to work through lunch."

"No." He squeezed me, his happy expression didn't slip so much as an inch. "You can choose the place, but no arguments."

"We'll see."

He hummed in his noncommittal

way that used to drive me crazy. Maybe it would, in a few more days, but right now, I'd let him get away with murder.

"Can I kiss you?"

I chuckled. "As if you've ever asked before."

"True," he said, smirking.

He ducked his head and captured my lips in the softest kiss I'd ever experienced. When he broke it, with that gentle smile teasing against my sensitive lips, I followed him, desperate for more.

"You can have anything you want, just do that again," I begged, my voice embarrassingly breathy.

"I'm going to hold you to that, Nymphy," he whispered before kissing me senseless again.

The heat of the lift spiralled with our desperation. I shrugged out of my blouse and started pawing at his chest, working to free his shirt from his trousers. His hands grasped at my bare skin, my breasts, my hips, my jaw, gliding up and down my body with a need I happily mirrored.

His lips feathered across my jaw to my neck, nipping teasingly at the sensitive area. I groaned and rose up on my toes, my hands sliding into his hair, urging him to do it again.

"I've missed you so fucking much," Matt whispered.

He edged me towards the wall of the elevator, his hands dipping lower and lower. My back bowed against the metal wall, the cold handrail pressing against me, setting off shivers.

"I missed you too." I smiled, surprised by the thrill of happiness those simple words sent through me.

His fingers trailed up my thigh, dragging my skirt with subtle scratches of his nails against my skin. I scrambled for his belt buckle and zipper. The fabric fell away, hitting the floor with barely a whisper of sound.

He teased me, toying with the edge of my underwear, never going far enough to provide more than a skitter of sensation.

Two can play this game.

I cupped him through his boxers, eliciting a pained groan. A grin stretched my lips while he buried his face in my neck, breathing harshly.

"If you want this to last, you might want to ease up."

My hand glided lower, cupping his balls, instead. His fingers tensed against my thigh and I barely resisted tensing in anticipation. When they pushed under the lacey fabric and into my heat, my head fell back as I groaned.

He worked me to the edge while my grip on his cock grew weaker through distraction. Then the pressure vanished completely and my moans turned to growls.

"Matt!" I panted. "Why did you stop?"

"Can't make everything easy for you, Nymphy." He tugged at the zipper on my skirt, applying teasing pressure with his fingers while he rid me of the skirt. His lust-filled green gaze lowered, scanning my almost bare body. "Besides, I couldn't enjoy the view."

My focus tracked the same path down his body. At least I'd managed to rid him of his trousers and shirt.

"Well, you've got your view now, so how about finishing what you started?" I bit my lip, considering the black boxers blocking *my* view. "And losing the boxers."

Matt stared at me, that smug smirk firmly in place while he pushed my patience to the brink. "Or I could keep teasing you…"

He lowered his head, his lips caressing lightly against mine and along my jaw. The tips of his fingers smoothed up my torso, tantalisingly slow and soft. My skin broke out in goose bumps and I shivered.

"We should be quick," I said, my voice breathy.

"Why?"

He rolled my nipple through the sheer fabric of my bra and I gasped.

"In case they get the doors open."

Matt hummed against my jaw. "Then they can watch you come."

"Hard to bloody do when you won't let me."

He chuckled. Then the sound cut off and a serious expression claimed his face. His hand pressed to my neck before he slammed his mouth down on mine. He kissed me hard and fast, all-consuming and combustible. Everything else ceased to exist.

My bra fell away, followed quickly by my underwear. My hands gripped his boxers, forcing the material down and his cock free between us. One graze of my finger and he pulled away, tutting.

"Patience," he whispered. His grin ruined the warning. "Don't move."

My body clenched at the order. I pressed my thighs together, willing the ache to ease while Matt grabbed his jacket off the floor. He retrieved a condom from his wallet, and then dropped everything else without a second glance. His lips found mine again as he tore the wrapper open.

Matt lifted one of my legs and I gripped the handrail with one hand. He pressed it to his hip, taking advantage to tease me with the broad head of his cock.

"Matt," I groaned. My eyes fluttered shut as need spiralled.

He thrust into me, tugging my hips forward until he bottomed out. For a second, we stood stock still, our foreheads pressed together, our breath escaping in ragged puffs, both of us shaking.

It had been so long since we'd had a moment like this and the need to relish everything rode through me. The way he stretched me, the way his hands caressed my skin lovingly no matter how rushed or rough we go, the quiet murmurs of praise falling from his lips almost unknown to him.

Then Matt moved, releasing the burn of need once more. He slammed into me over and over again, forcing my body to the edge so fast it stole my breath.

My eyes fell shut while I begged him to let me go.

They snapped open again at a sharp sting at the base of my scalp. Matt's smouldering gaze fixed on me.

"Eyes. On. Me," he panted with each thrust.

And then my orgasm hit, tearing a cry from my throat. Matt swallowed the sound with his lips. He continued to thrust into me, his voice and rhythm growing shakier by the second.

"Fucking hell, Daphne," he shouted as my core tightened around him.

His hips jolted and he buried his face in my neck again. His movements slowed, but each shift of his cock inside of my triggered aftershocks, perpetually keeping me on the edge of intense pleasure.

I stared at the wall over Matt's shoulder, dazed.

Had it always been this good?

We lay on the floor, cushioned by our clothing. Our chests rose and fell fast while our skin glittered beneath the mirrored ceiling.

"I can't believe we did that in work," I whispered, my gaze fixed on my very unperturbed face in the reflection above.

My cheeks were red, but I couldn't blame embarrassment. The smile on my lips screamed a level of satisfaction you couldn't get from anything but orgasmic bliss.

"I can't believe a routine meeting turned into this." He turned his head and studied me with something close to wonder. "I didn't think you'd ever give me a second chance. I'm not sure how I got so lucky without…" He returned his focus to the ceiling, a frown now marring his brow.

"Without sharing all of your secrets?"

He nodded, catching my eye in the

mirror. Indecision danced across his face before clearing entirely.

"This stays between us."

I turned on my side at the serious tone in his voice. "What does?"

He rolled towards me, chewing his lip. His hand brushed along my side and up to my face.

"If they'd found out you knew, they would have blacklisted you. I couldn't risk it, especially not when I knew I was leaving." His fingers caressed my cheek. "I wouldn't have been there to protect you and once you found out…"

Was he saying what I thought he was saying?

"What about your NDA?"

Amusement fluttered through me at his sudden willingness to share. If I'd thought sex would encourage him to break his silence, I would have tried it years ago.

"I need to earn your trust again. It wouldn't be right for me to expect you to be open with me and not return the favour." His lips quirked in a self-depreciating smile. "That would be an old Matt move, right?"

Should I stop him?

He barrelled on before I could make up my mind.

"Just before you applied to Cleo Records, a raft of sexual harassment and assault allegations came to light." He studied my face. What he searched for I couldn't tell and the silence prickled at my skin.

"Why would that cause an NDA?"

"The allegations were against the owner's son." His expression hardened. "They paid the women off and made everyone in the building sign an NDA, whether they knew why or not."

Matt smoothed a finger along my jaw. His gaze softened on me, but some of the darkness remained. He didn't need to tell me he'd imagined what might have happened had I ended up working there. The horror of it darkened his eyes.

"We're talking about a suave rich guy who was raised to believe he could have anything he wanted. Refusals be damned." He shuffled closer, pressing his forehead to mine, the remembered heartbreak painted plain on his face. "Do you see why I had to keep you away no matter the cost to me, to us?"

Cleo Records must have become a lawless hunting ground for the asshole. NDAs in that situation achieved two things: silencing everyone who could warn new female staff and creating a safe space for him to attack people without fear of repercussions.

No wonder Matt hadn't wanted me in the company. Had I gotten under his radar, no one would have protected me.

He wouldn't have stopped either. Once a predator, always a predator.

The thought that more women had fallen victim to him in the last five years made me queasy.

"Unsurprisingly, I do." I smiled despite the sadness laying heavy on my heart. "I don't know how I would have reacted if you'd told me the truth back then, but I appreciate that you have now. Those poor women."

His hand coasted down my bare arm and he wove our fingers together.

"I'm so sorry I hurt you," he whispered, his voice hitching with emotion.

"Matt, it's okay. I understand now." I squeezed his hand, forcing any sadness about what might have been, both good and bad, to the back of my mind. "Today, we start from zero."

"You're sure you can let it go?"

"Already have."

He hesitated for all of a second before that brilliant smile overtook his face again. He leaned in and his lips grazed mine softly.

"Are you guys still good in there?" The disembodied voice of the security man asked, interrupting the beginnings of a sweet kiss.

Disappointment skittered through me as Matt scrambled to his feet.

Stop it. This isn't the end of anything.

It's the start.

He flipped the phone panel open and fumbled for the phone, almost dropping it in his haste.

"Yes, we're good but boiling. What's the verdict?"

I strained to hear any tonal suggestions that he knew what we'd been up to while confined. He just sounded flat and concerned.

"The maintenance crew just arrived," his voice continued to blare from the surround speakers. "You're stuck between floors, so they're going to get the doors open and pull you out. We'll be about five minutes."

"Okay, thank you."

Matt placed the phone back and turned to me, his expression stunned. He glanced between my very naked body and the clothes littering the lift floor.

"I guess we'd better get dressed."

I pointed at him, a frown wiping out my bliss. "What's with the face?"

"I can't believe we're actually getting out of here." He leaned down and offered me his hand. "I almost don't want to leave." A devilish smirk curved his lips. "Do you think he'd stall them, if we asked nicely?"

"You're incorrigible." I laughed before sliding my hand into his. "How about we get dressed and hope no one finds out that we christened the lift?"

"As if one of them hasn't purposefully pulled the emergency alarm before." He snorted. "Daph, we deal with rock stars."

He had a point.

CHAPTER SIX

Free of the lift, I rushed into my office to change out my suit, Matt following closely behind.

"Don't you have a meeting to get to?" I asked as I shimmied out of my clothes for the second time in an hour.

"Hank can wait another ten minutes." He shrugged while his gaze turned heated and lowered, devouring my exposed skin.

"Keep those looks to yourself, mister." Laughing, I buttoned the new, gutter-water free blouse with quick fingers. "I've got a rock star waiting to be raked through the coals."

He hummed in agreement but his

eyes continued to follow my shifting hands. "So lunch after you're done?"

"It's good to know you can still be that single-minded." I chuckled at him as I shrugged into my fresh jacket. "Let's get our meetings done and I'll see what I can do."

He smirked. "I'll be done in ten. Make yours quick and I'll treat you to Frederick's."

"You don't need to bribe me to have lunch with you."

I picked up my phone, barely holding back a giddy squeal. I loved Frederick's and he knew it. They had the best dessert. The rest of their food was amazing too, but dessert.

His brows rose and he crossed his arms. "Then I can make a reservation for The Caterpillar…"

My eyes narrowed on him. "Stop messing with me."

"Maybe I'm not." Amusement shone in his green eyes. "Maybe your tastes have changed and you actually like the Cat now."

Even saying the name of that

restaurant made me shiver in disgust. They had rave reviews. He begged me to go when we were first dating. Then it gave me food poisoning, and I never went back.

"Book Frederick's please."

A knock sounded on my door before he could voice his teasing satisfaction. Ivy popped her head in, her blonde hair perfectly straight, unlike mine. My raven locks probably resembled a bird's nest by that point.

"Casey Jackson just checked in downstairs," she said, while I dug around in my bag for a brush to smooth out the knots in my hair.

"Right, on my way." I forced the brush through my hair, then dropped it on my desk and started scraping my hair back into a smoother bun. "Give me half an hour, Matt, and we'll leave."

"Sure thing, Nymphy." I could hear his smirk without lifting my head. He'd probably already made reservations.

Ivy's gaze shifted between the two

of us with unmasked curiosity. I shook my head at her as I brushed past and into the hall.

"Did we delay him, or is he just late?"

"Late, of course," she muttered and fell into step next to me. "If you're busy, I could handle this one." She glanced over her shoulder and I followed her gaze to find Matt watching my brisk walk to the elevator banks.

"Thanks, but I'll just make it quick."

We stopped in the marble-encased entrance hall and Ivy wasted no time shooting me more questioning looks.

"Will you stop that? I've got work to do."

"You're not going to fool me, chickie. You could handle Casey Jackson in your sleep." She crossed her arms and fixed me with her impatient gaze. "Gimme the deets."

The old-fashioned dials above the lift started counting up. Ivy frowned at it before taking a step closer to me, her eyes widening with urgency.

"Make it quick, or I'll get it out of him." She pointed over my shoulder.

"Fine," I sighed and ducked my head closer to hers. "He's my ex from five years ago."

"Wait!" Her eyes widened and she hissed, "You mean he's the one who screwed you out of a job? Why would you take him back?"

"We don't have time for this." I glanced at the quickly approaching lift. "It wasn't all as it seemed, and you'll have to be patient for the rest."

I turned around, finding Matt still watching me from my office doorway. He looked happily dazed, an expression I probably mirrored when not being questioned by Daphne.

"I mean looking at that bod, I'd forgive him too." She tilted her head.

I chuckled as I elbowed her. "Don't say that so loudly. He'll get ideas."

"What kind of ideas?" she asked, smirking.

The lift pinged before I could do more than blush. Matt's focus drifted over my shoulder.

"Well, hello ladies," an annoyingly familiar British voice said behind me. "If I'd known Hank had rolled out the red carpet, I would have been on time."

Recognition flared in Matt's eyes. I arched a questioning brow at him, but he only had eyes for Casey.

Then two things happened at once: Matt's expression darkened, and Casey draped his arms across mine and Ivy's shoulders.

I ignored the creepy sensation it inspired and pasted a polite smile to my lips. I had a job to do.

"Mr Jackson, thank you for joining us." Shrugging him off, I turned and cast a cursory glance over his bedraggled appearance.

You'd think the man had just rolled out of bed. His mousy brown hair stood on end while his t-shirt appeared twisted in places, as if he'd thrown it back on after someone ripped it off him. If I were being marched in to plead my case after months of escalating destruction, I'd at least shower and change my clothes. The man had to think himself untouchable.

"We'll be meeting in the main conference room." I glanced pointedly at the empty space behind him. "Is your legal consul running late?"

"There's no need for formalities." Casey held his arms out, an attempt at a sultry smile tugging at his lips. His gaze dropped to my chest. "Call me Casey, gorgeous."

"*Mr Jackson,* I must advise you to have your own legal representative present."

"I'm sure we can work this out without all of that. After all, it was just a small window."

My lips flatlined. "That's funny. I, and the venue, would call it a historic stained-glass window that stretched over ten feet." I turned on my heel and gestured for him to precede me down the hall.

"Oh, after you," he said with massive grin.

Casey shuffled in close, trying to crowd me in a way he never had before. I'd dealt with his misdemeanours for years and the company had mostly shrugged it off as just another rock star being a rock star.

Something had changed recently. His acts of destruction were escalating, catching people in the crosshairs. We hadn't just pulled him for breaking a window. The method of destruction that concerned us far more.

"You know where the conference room is. I'll meet you there in a moment with the tapes."

"I'm sure there's no need for tapes." He fixed that suave smile firmly back in place. "We could work something out, right, love?" His tone made it clear that he expected me to fall over at his thinly veiled offer for sex. Instead, I grimaced.

He wound an arm around my waist, without so much as pausing to consider.

"No." I pushed hard against him and he stumbled back with pure astonishment sweeping across his face.

A door had opened down the hall

just as Casey grabbed me. Unfortunately for Casey, Hank, the head of TPI stepped into the hall and started towards us, his brows risen, silently questioning whether I needed backup. Then his attention rose over my shoulder, and my stomach inexplicably dropped.

"Keep your fucking hands off my girlfriend, Michael," Matt shouted.

Michael?

Casey moved away from me, turning to face a very angry Matt.

"Matt, nice to see you're still in business." Casey attempted to look sad but failed to mask the malicious gleam in his eyes. "Dad thought for sure you'd fail when you left Cleo."

When you left Cleo…

They clearly knew each other, but my files on Casey had never mentioned the name Michael or that he had some connection to Cleo Records.

"Apparently nothing changes in this industry." Matt glared at Casey, his entire body tensing up. "Problematic assholes can recreate themselves with fake names, and the rest of us soldier on, blinded by our love for music and hope that the system will change."

And then it clicked.

"It's him, isn't it?" I asked Matt, shock raising my voice.

Matt nodded.

"Come on, love, you'd have loved a spin on this." He gestured to his cock and I just about threw up. "All those money-grabbing whores loved it before they…"

"Don't finish that sentence," I hissed.

"Aw, I knew you had a thing for me, gorgeous."

Then he moved in so fast, he caught me off guard and kissed me. Right in front of Matt and my boss, *his* boss. Shock froze me to the spot but my lack of action didn't matter. Casey was pulled away from me just as fast as he'd approached.

The hard sound of a fist connecting with skin snapped me from my horror. Casey hit the ground, groaning, while Matt stood over him with a face like thunder, clenching his fists as though he wanted him to get back up so he could have another go.

"Matt! My office," Hank ordered, his voice booming down the hall. "Now."

"Now you're in trouble, Mattie boy." Casey laughed, the sound gurgling as blood ran from his nose. "Never did like that the ladies loved me more, did you?"

"We'll see how much they love you when your vile affection for sexual assault gets out to your fans." Matt stepped over him, following Hank to his office without so much as a glance back.

I rushed after them, Casey could be dealt with another time. If he were even my problem after today.

Hank took his seat with a grim expression as I entered his office. I shut the door and he ordered the whole story out of Matt. He glanced at me, old hesitation in his eyes. I nodded, urging him on. Slowly he opened up, sharing every detail he could recall from Cleo Records, the owner's reaction to sweep it under a rug and pay off the victims the moment whispers began to circle the office. How he sent Michael away in an attempt to save his reputation and the company but failed.

When Matt fell silent, Hank shifted his focus to me. "Can't say I'm all that surprised given the escalations of late. What's your take on this, Daphne?"

I sank into a chair next to Matt, my brow puckering in confusion. "In what way?"

"How would you advise we react?"

I sat back hard in my chair. He really should have called the more experienced legal team in, but his gaze remained fixed on me, unwavering.

"For the sake of the company, I'd suggest nullifying his contracts effective immediately and distancing the company from him." I chewed my lip, trying to remember the clauses worked into each artists contract. "Given we brought Casey— uh, Michael?—in today because he threw his guitar tech through a window, I don't believe his legal team would advise him to take legal action against us or Matt for breaking his NDA."

He nodded, his expression solemn. "I agree. What about the victims?"

"I think that's entirely up to you." My hands twisted in my lap, the weight of the situation settling hard on my shoulders. "You could check for whispers within the company and arrange therapy? But I'm not sure what we could do for those from Cleo Records. We may need to see how things unravel once his contract is cancelled."

Again he nodded. "Would you advise notifying the press as to the reason?" His hand hovered over the phone, ready to put my advice into action far too quickly for my peace of mind.

"I think that's a question for your public relations team."

Matt's warm hand landed on top of mine, stopping my fidgeting. I smiled at him, grateful for the support.

"Whether you divulge his past should be debated with them and the higher legal team." I wrapped my hands around Matt's, squeezing. "But we'd certainly be within our right to share his long list of failings as Casey Jackson."

"Agreed."

He picked up the phone, hit three and waved us off. I stood, reeling from the events of the day.

"I have one demand before we go, Hank," Matt said, standing with me.

Hank glanced up at him, his brows raised in question.

"Daphne goes nowhere near him from now on. I'm calling what happened out there assault." He pointed to the door. "If he's still in the building, I want him escorted out by security, and I don't want her anywhere near this as it unfolds."

Hank's gaze shifted between us, curiosity slowly filtering in to ease the severity of his expression.

"One second," he muttered into the phone before grinning at us, completely breaking from the severe CEO for a moment. "Well, well, this I didn't expect. I absolutely agree with you, Matt. Consider it done."

Matt nodded and Hank went back to his call. With that dismissal, we left.

The door shut behind us and I collapsed against the wall. "I don't understand how the day ended up like this."

He leaned against the wall next to me, a soft smile on his lips. "Some good I hope?"

I smiled, acknowledging the truth of it. The day had started out drastically wrong. I definitely couldn't have predicted that something so inconsequential but annoying would start a chain of events that would give me a second chance at love with Matt.

Or that those events would start a course of punishment for the person who had been the driving force in my five years of misdirected ire.

"Yes, some good," I whispered before rising on my tiptoes and pressing a soft kiss to his lips.

His hands rested on my waist, the warmth of such a basic touch another reminder of how safe he made me feel.

He kissed me back slowly, like we had all the time in the world and not five long years to make up for.

He pulled back, a teasing light in his eyes. "So lunch?"

$\mathcal{M}$att held true to his word, whisking me straight out of the office and to Frederick's. I'd like to say I was surprised to find the maître d' expecting us, but that would be a lie. In the five months we dated, he had always been a stickler for making appointments and keeping them, whether they were a dinner reservation or a promise to call after a gig in another city.

My brows rose at the bottle of expensive champagne waiting in an ice bucket on our table next to bushy white laurel flowers. Matt chuckled as he pulled out my chair. Since our first date, he'd loved to tease me with hints of my name's origin, the Greek goddess Daphne. The fact he knew about the flowers or had requested them didn't surprise me.

When did he have time to organise all of this?

Then he sat down opposite me, smirk firmly in place.

"We're celebrating. Of course I called ahead."

I pulled out one of his tricks, humming noncommittally. He laughed harder.

"Alright, so I have an organisation addiction." He shrugged. "Not going to change it any time soon. Besides, you love it."

"Maybe," I whispered.

"No maybe about it, Nymphy. You hate being the organised one." He popped the cork on the champagne, masking my gasp.

"Can you not say that so loudly?" I hissed, leaning over the table. "I'm a lawyer, I'm meant to thrive on order."

He handed me a glass, grin firmly in place.

"The state of your office at the end of the week wouldn't be a secret." He sipped his drink, his eyes shone with mirth over the rim. "I'm sure you're a great lawyer. Hank trusts you, whether your office is a state or not. A little chaos doesn't change that."

"Very true." I took a sip of the fizzy liquid, studying his smiling face. "I can concede that your organised habits will benefit me."

"How so?"

"When do you rejoin the tour?"

His smile fell.

"Yes, I'm aware Rhiannon is currently in the middle of a European tour." I glanced at my watch and the date listed. "It's April. From what I heard the tour ends in July. When do you head out again?"

"I forgot how straight to the point you could be." Matt rubbed his jaw, his lips slowly curling again. "I leave tomorrow, which is why I didn't want to wait for lunch."

Most people would feel panicked or upset that he hadn't mentioned it before gaining himself a second chance. Not me. I'd always known how our relationship would unfold. A band manager must travel, and with Rhiannon only now blowing up, Matt wouldn't want to miss a second of it.

"Okay." I nodded. "So what's your plan?"

He blinked at me.

"What? We went through this five years ago."

"I know." He chuckled. "I just didn't expect you to be so accepting so fast I guess."

"It's your job and your passion, Matt." I tilted my head, studying his serious expression with a self-satisfied smile. "We wouldn't be able to make this work if I didn't appreciate it."

"Very true." He put down his glass and leaned forward, resting his elbows on the table. His knee bumped my leg beneath the table, the brief contact tuning every nerve in my body to him.

"We're on tour until the end of July, and then the guys are moving home to Wales. If you have any leave to use, you could meet us for long weekends. I'll arrange all the transport."

"If you send me some dates, I can talk to Hank."

He picked up his phone, pressed a button and then my phone pinged. I smirked when I glanced at the preview on my screen. A list of dates, two a month, it seemed.

"When did you have time to pull that together?" Amusement dripped from my voice.

"I didn't." He grinned as my brows furrowed. "I took on Ryan's girlfriend as my assistant for the tour. She runs a tighter ship than I do."

"Not possible." I laughed. "No one is more anal than you."

He shrugged. "You'll just have to make your judgement when you meet her." He reached across the table, his expression shifting to a more serious edge as he took my hand. "I know it'll take time for us to get back to where we were," Matt said, "but I'm so happy we have the chance to try."

Considering six hours ago, I thought I hated him, I shouldn't have felt so light and carefree with him. Perspective and knowledge changed everything. I'd lost him once because I refused to trust him to look out for me. I wouldn't repeat the same mistake again. Hopefully, he'd learned to.

"We'll figure things out as we go. We're both busy people, Matt. We knew always knew getting time together would take work." I squeezed his hand. "I'm here to work for it. I think I have enough leave to do at least a weekend a month, if not more. There's always video calls in-between." I widened my eyes suggestively.

"Yes, there definitely is." A mischievous light entered his eyes. "I had to listen to Ryan on the phone to Alys for at least a month. Oh, the payback will be sweet."

I snorted. "He won't know what hit him."

His gaze zeroed in on me. "We can start tomorrow."

"Matt, be serious. We're trying to lay down plans."

He nodded fast. "This is part of the plans."

For a couple of seconds, we stared at each other, him deadly serious but eager, and me biting back a smile. How had I ever forgotten how fun he could be?

"Fine, one payback call." I pointed at him, forcing a stern expression I didn't feel. "Then you find spaces away from the band to call me." He started grinning the second I agreed, and I had my doubts as to whether he'd heard the rest. "I'm serious, Matt. I have to meet these people multiple times. One call within earshot, and from then on, you call me in private."

He nodded, lifting my hand to his lips. "Deal, Nymphy."

Matt kissed the palm of my hand and my heart decided any resistance ended now.

He spent most of his time deadly

serious, but there were always these sweet moments. He'd be goofy and teasing. He'd wind me up, knowing full well he was winding me up but pretend he wasn't.

Then he'd make the most romantic gestures, flowers appearing without warning or cause on my doorstep, phone calls when he ran late. He always collated information, digging for my favourite anything with little effort and using it to bring me even a minute of joy on an unexpected day.

I'd never met another man like him and probably never would.

"Now, shall we order or do you want to pretend we ate and go back to my place?" Matt's heated gaze bore into mine and my core ached at the suggestion.

Second chances were rare.

This time, I needed to hold on tight and embrace every second. No running when life didn't quite work out right.

"Let's go."

urn the page for an excerpt from Chasing Alys, book one in the True Platinum series following Rhiannon, the band Matt manages.

CHASING
alys
TRUE PLATINUM SERIES
MORGANA
BEVAN

Music blared from every direction, deafening the eclectic mix of people crammed into the dark, modest bar. Most ignored the band prancing around the small stage, choosing to shout at their neighbour between winces instead. Some crowded the bar itself, while others stood in groups on the dance floor before the stage. Almost all of them wore black band t-shirts and jeans. I'd missed the memo on the t-shirts, but then, I didn't own any. My green blouse would have to do.

There were other women going against the uniform who stuck out worse than me. A dark dive bar didn't seem like the place for short dresses, stilettos or faces caked with make-up, but then, it wasn't my scene, so what did I know?

As far as I was concerned, heels would just stick to the dirty rubber floor. The air was so stagnant and hot that sweat dripped down the walls. My face already felt like it was melting, and I wore only a thin layer of foundation. I hated to think about the time these girls had wasted perfecting their eyeliner and the curve of their lashes. It would all end up nothing more than a black streak down their cheeks in a couple of hours.

I pressed my spine into the pillar between the bar and the stairs leading down to the entrance. Then I remembered the sweat coating the walls and shot away before it could seep into my blouse. It was the perfect vantage spot. Emily wouldn't be able to miss me when she finally turned up.

After scanning the growing crowd for what felt like the hundredth time, I took a deep glug of wine and grimaced, fighting an instant need to spit it out. Served in a plastic pint glass, I'd naively thought it couldn't get worse. But the burn in my throat begged to differ. *That's what I get for drinking wine from a bar that smells like stale beer.*

Had the music been better, this gig might have turned the tide on my distaste for live music. There was a crowd, but it wasn't claustrophobic. I still wouldn't be able to have a conversation without losing my voice the next day, but at least I didn't feel like there was no escape.

Thirty minutes passed. My feet stuck to the floor, my ears felt like they were bleeding, my taste buds were a thing of the past, and Emily was nowhere to be seen. I couldn't even get drunk to drown out the screams of the man on stage who had forgotten how to produce words.

Foot tapping against the disgusting floor, I glared at the gaunt figure holding the microphone. He needed a haircut and an introduction to running water. Long black strands stuck to his thin body – *when had he lost his shirt?* – and it had nothing to do with sweat. That shine seemed far too pronounced.

Reverb squawked through the small space, and I winced in tandem with the rest of the crowd. Why had I given in to Emily so quickly yesterday? I should have argued, resisted for at least an hour.

I lived with Emily and when production was in full swing, we didn't see each other much. A production coordinator's day started far earlier than a school counsellor's, and it ended much later. That meant we only caught sight of each other when I had a down day, which was few and far between. If my day off didn't fall on a weekend, the most we managed was sharing a meal. Yet despite being like passing ships most days, we could still read each other with very little effort.

I don't know how I'd survived without my wayward best friend for the first eleven years of my life. Her attaching herself to me had been the best thing to happen, and not only because she ran off a bully with the whack of a textbook. She'd made life more exciting in our tiny village. Of the two of us, she was the daring one. She'd climb forty-foot trees on the regular, getting stuck almost every time. People would tell her she wasn't allowed to do something, and she'd defy them all.

Back then, I'd wished she'd approach love with the same daredevil outlook. I'd thought she was missing out. Now I knew better.

My eyes strayed to the entrance yet again – and snagged on an oddly familiar blond-haired man. He stood on the opposite side of the room, staring at me whilst surrounded by a group of men. All four of them were varying degrees of hot, and together they packed an effective punch. Around them, men outright gawked and women tried to catch their eyes.

Not a single one of their watchers approached, though. Nothing but empty space surrounded them, and except for Blondie, they seemed oblivious, laughing and joking with each other. The four of them were chiselled, over six foot tall, and gave off an air of unaffected calm in the face of so much attention. I could understand why they pulled focus; they were the epitome of cool and confident.

Despite their competing good looks, my gaze kept coming back to the blond-haired one. His friends chattered around him, but he was silent, oblivious to them. His expression was oddly restrained as he stared at me across the smoky room. His face tickled my memories, but I couldn't pinpoint why he seemed familiar. His hair fell to his shoulders in effortless waves that would make any woman envious.

Then his eyes snared mine, pulling me in until the music faded. An easy smile tipped up the edges of his lips, and my heart beat faster. An image of him walking down the stairs towards me last night popped into my head. What were the chances that I'd stumble upon him twice in two nights?

He looked different with his long hair falling in messy waves. Last night he'd been cleaner cut with his hair pulled back. He'd been hot then, but this…

Glancing away, he raised a bottle to his lips and my eyes dipped, taking in the tight swimmer's build hidden beneath his plain white t-shirt and black jeans. His trousers moulded to his thighs, and the shirt was so thin he might as well have been topless. If I'd met him last year, I might have taken it as an invitation.

Why did I remember him? I was usually terrible with faces, and our interaction had lasted a matter of seconds.

I caught my gaze before it could fall further and forced my attention back to his face. His lips twitched and my face warmed. He'd caught my once-over. Still, I couldn't look away. I didn't think I'd ever grow tired of that smile.

A tall, thin guy covered in tattoos turned to follow the direction of his stare. He smirked, slapping my watcher on the back before leaning in. His lips moved, and the pair laughed. He gave him a shove towards me, and my stomach dropped. Looking was one thing, but being approached in this dive bar was not on my agenda. I didn't care how he made my pulse race; I was done with men.

I tore my eyes away and unlocked my phone to check messages, social media – anything to distract me. When my eyes tipped up again, drawn to him by some cruel magnetic force, he was openly grinning at me from across the room.

Heat suffused my body, and I willed it away. All of my attempts to let people in had backfired. I was tired of trying, of getting my heart broken. And I was sick of men taking advantage and treating me like their plaything. After my last mishap, it was becoming clear that true happiness would not include a man. I wasn't sure I wanted it to, anyway.

A nice house with Emily close by would do me fine.

I frowned at my phone. It revealed no more clues than the strangers surrounding me. It wasn't like her to ditch me without at least a text, and Emily hadn't been online in four hours. My fingers hovered over the keyboard while I chewed my lip in indecision. She hadn't seen my last ten messages either. This was not like her.

Fuck it. Another text couldn't hurt.

Alys: Where are you? Gig's started and the wine sucks. HURRY UP! Xxx

I stared at the screen for another minute out of some misguided hope that little speech bubbles would appear. They didn't.

"You've either been stood up or your friends are late," someone shouted above me. Air tickled my ear. The sound startled me enough that I added my foul wine to the sticky cocktail coating the old rubber floor.

My head snapped up. The god from across the room grinned down at me, his crystal-blue eyes captivating. His slightly crooked smile jump-started my pulse, and my grip on common sense slipped.

I frowned at his nose. *Not quite a god.* The tiny bump on the bridge would have ruled him out of godhood.

"None of the above?" He leaned towards me to be heard over the cater-wauling filtering through the amps. His trim body blocked out the stage, and I couldn't find it in me to be mad about it.

My lungs filled with his smoulder-ing, spicy scent, and if I weren't a trained dancer, my knees might have buckled. *What the utter hell?*

Eyes narrowed, I considered his open, patient face. There were two kinds of attractive men: the ones who were oblivious to their power, and the ones who knew their effect and ex-ploited it.

This guy knew he was good look-ing, and he expected me to fall at his feet. I should have spotted it last night. I'd had enough experience with his type over the years to know that I hated that kind of man. They were always looking for better, and they had a nasty habit of disappearing right when your heart decided it was safe to let them in.

And yet that smile and those eyes still held me. I couldn't make myself turn away. "My friend's late."

"Remind me to thank her," he shouted.

A small part of me was grateful for my three-inch boots. With men over six foot, they made the height difference far more manageable. His eyes bore into mine, fixated. I could feel the heat radiating off his body, and my lower belly clenched in response. Hate these men or not, my body couldn't ignore their charm.

I'd dated a lot over the years – set-ups, online matches, one-night stands, unwise attempts at relationships – but none of them had made the room fade or my throat close up with nerves. Not even one of them had captivated me with nothing but a smile or made my heart race with the caress of their gaze. Somehow this one cut through the disinterest. I frowned.

"So, this is going to sound crazy, but you seem really familiar," he said.

Relief snatched my unwanted nerves. I wasn't odd for remembering such a brief encounter. "We passed each other on the stairs last night at the Old Ballroom."

His shoulders relaxed at my response. That easy smile creased his eyes, and my chest tightened. "We did, but I don't think that's it."

I searched his face for clues. I'd have remembered meeting him before yesterday. No way would I forget his quiet confidence or my inexplicable fascination with the quirk of his lips.

"You were on the set of the *Mystery Lines* show this summer, right?"

I nodded. I'd been on it since May, rode out an uneasy couple of weeks short of production staff and still produced what would hopefully be the next contender for an Emmy or BAFTA.

He raised the bottle to his lips, grinning. "I thought so."

My brows creased as I searched my memories from the summer. I couldn't place him on my set. I would have noticed him.

"My mate, Shaun Martin, was in it. You're the woman who told the crew off for being callous idiots."

I covered my face, shaking my head. "You saw that?"

Callused fingers gently pulled my hand away from my eyes. "Don't be embarrassed. It was brilliant. They all stood about while the chaperone tried to get a handle on that little girl. You jumped right in and calmed her down."

"She was going blue in the face. Someone had to do something before she passed out."

"And that someone was you?"

"No one else had the sense to, so yeah, it had to be me." My throat hurt from shouting, but I didn't want to stop talking to him.

"I left the set pretty fast. How did

they all take it?" he asked, rocking back on his heels while I squirmed with re-membered embarrassment.

"My production manager found it funny. The rest of them tiptoed around me for a couple of days." I watched the swirl of wine in my plastic cup while I spoke.

"It was brave," he said, his tone firm.

I peeked at him from beneath my lashes. His eyes travelled across my face, seeming to absorb every detail. "You think so?"

He nodded. "Hundred percent."

"Did Shaun Martin really see?" I asked, my voice tentative and barely audible. He stared at my lips, frowning as he tried to decipher my question.

Shaun Martin was the leading man of the series and kind of a big deal, even if he had started out trying to tank his career. At the beginning of production for *Mystery Lines*, he'd tried to get plenty of people fired. He hadn't been successful, and thankfully he'd gotten over whatever had been making him act out. But I'd still disrupted set, even if I was defending a helpless girl. Someone like him hated wasting time, and I'm sure he could talk a producer into giving him anything he wanted the next time around, including not hiring a brazen production coordinator.

The frown cleared and Blondie's amused eyes were appraising when they jumped back to mine. "He thought it was impressive too. His assistant was quite the firecracker. You gave her a run for her money."

"You met Mona?"

He nodded. "A couple of times now. Do you know her well?"

I shrugged. "A little. I hired her."

His unfocused eyes shifted to the left. "When she was trying to get out from under Shaun, you mean?"

"I didn't know they were involved at the time, but I guess so."

Our production secretary quit without notice two months in. She'd been missed, and the production team had struggled to absorb her tasks. For a couple weeks, we floundered trying to keep on top of the last-minute transport and accommodation changes for the entire cast and crew, as well as prepare the sides for the next day. When Mona accepted my offer to jump ship and join production, I snapped her up without much thought. Thankfully, Shaun hadn't been pissed, and it hadn't backfired on me.

"Did you find out why she was crying?" he asked, bringing me back to the present.

I frowned at the sudden question. My mind raced, trying to figure out how it applied to Mona. I'd never seen her cry.

"What?"

"The girl." His intense blue eyes snared me like a trap. *Why do I feel the urge to spill all my secrets to this guy every time our eyes meet?* "Did you find out why she was upset?"

The genuine interest in his gaze both intrigued and terrified me. Men rarely cared about my job. They asked the perfunctory questions about meeting famous people, but their eyes always glazed over when I tried to go deeper. Not this guy. I liked it too much.

"She missed her mother. She died a couple of months before, and it was her first acting gig without her." A pang hit me in the chest. I tried to force that memory out of my mind by raising the awful wine to my mouth and focusing on the acidic liquid searing my taste buds. It didn't help.

Our only child actress had thrown a fit because no one had danced her around the space or read lines with her. Like her mother did and never would again.

His amusement faded. "Poor kid." Admiration filled his tone when he added: "I've never seen someone soothe a kid so fast. Good work."

Heat spread up my neck and into my cheeks.

"Hey, don't be embarrassed. It took guts." He raised his drink to his lips without breaking eye contact. "There were loads of people there whose job it was to look after the kid, right?"

"Yes, but I went about it wrong. I should have spoken to the director and had him step in." But I hadn't really been thinking. I'd heard her cry and reacted.

"Your way was far more badass." He smiled. My lips curved in response. "I'm sorry for staring. I guess your face stuck with me after that."

I nodded. My eyes drifted towards the stairs, hoping Emily would magically appear and let me escape his sincere light. But no luck. Emily was still MIA and this guy still drew me in. *So much for dousing the flames.*

For the first time, I noticed the sound engineer glaring with his arms crossed at the idiot on stage swinging the mic at the very tip of safe. *Somebody really should stop him before he hits someone.* Hell, if it meant he'd stop screaming, I'd do it. There was screamo and then there was this ear-destroying monstrosity. There were plenty of leather-wearing men in the room sporting spiky jewellery who probably loved it, but even they frowned at the band.

"Do you like this type of music?" My persistent companion shouted. He tapped my arm with his cold plastic bottle, drawing my attention back to him. Goose bumps broke out, raising the hairs on my skin.

"How can you call this noise music?" I asked, pretending that I knew enough about it to have an opinion beyond the Top 40.

He shrugged. "Some people like it."

"But not you?" I held my breath, hopeful I'd at last found some reason to push him away.

"Definitely not me. I like my music to have understandable lyrics."

Relief coursed through me before I could squash it. So maybe I didn't want him to leave. My eyes widened as they travelled between the stage and him. "That has lyrics?"

He chuckled. "They say it does. I have my doubts."

I glanced over his shoulder at his

friends. They were engrossed in a heated argument and seemingly oblivious to his absence. They gestured wildly between them, their faces animated and invested.

"What's that about?" I asked, nodding towards them.

"Who knows. Jared probably said something to wind them up." He pointed over his shoulder. "That's normal. I'm far more interested in you."

I laughed. "Smooth."

He ran his free hand through his hair, grinning boyishly at me. "I'm not all that great with that kind of thing."

I snorted and his lips widened, revealing a flash of his teeth.

"I'd rather not get drawn into whatever they're arguing about. Would you mind if I kept hanging out with you?" The words hit me as effectively as if he'd whispered them in my ear.

The answer should have been no, instantaneous and swift rolling off my lips. I wasn't interested in taking this brief flirtation further. I definitely didn't want to lead anyone on. Yet I smiled and nodded.

Relief slivered across his face before his confident demeanour fell back into place.

"If you could have dinner with only two of your favourite artists, who would you pick?" His eyes wandered across my face, taking in my surprise. "What? Were you expecting me to ask something else?"

"Maybe."

"I'll tell you mine if you tell me yours."

I shook my head, unsure if he meant my pick of artists or the question I'd expected to fall from his lips. Surprising man wasn't so straightforward.

"You don't want to know the answer," I said.

"Fair warning. If you say Matthew Tuck from Bullet for My Valentine, I'm going to call you a hypocrite." His eyes sparkled, and a ridiculous thrill swept through me. I enjoyed him looking at me with that teasing glint.

I'd heard of Bullet for My Valentine. I'd have to live in a cave not to have. They were a Welsh band from a couple towns over, but I had no idea what they sounded like. "Okay. You still don't want to hear my answer."

He stepped closer and his face lit up. He laughed at me. "Now I need to know. It can't be that bad. You don't look like the sort to love teeny-bopper music."

I laughed too, basking in his attention despite myself. "I'd probably invite Halsey and the Ward Thomas sisters."

He pointed at me. "That's three."

"I can't exactly split up the Ward Thomas sisters."

"Then you need to pick just them."

"Or I could pick someone else."

He gestured for me to do so.

"Tanc Sade."

He frowned, focusing on a point beyond me. "He's not a musician."

"He played one."

"Yes, but he's not a real musician." He smirked, shaking his head. "You're terrible at this game," he said, raising the bottle to his lips.

"I did warn you."

He laughed, the sound rushing around me in a rare break in the music and drawing an uncontrollable smile from me. I could feel my resolve weakening. It would be wise to leave before I forgot why I needed a break from men in the first place. My eyes strayed to the stairs, but I stayed rooted to the spot. *Just a few more minutes.*

Find Chasing Alys on your favourite online retailer or request it from your local library or bookstore today.
books2read.com/ChasingAlys

Consider this your introduction to the True Platinum brand. You've met three of Rhiannon's band members, but there's still one more to come and even more bands to join the lineup.

Here's the list of books in the True Platinum series, current and to-be-released:

Chasing Alys - Book 1

When love's song takes over, you're forced to find the beat.

Once a player, always a player. And all men, in my experience, are. It's like they can't help themselves.

Usually, that reminder is enough. I dismiss most before I even meet them. Especially the hot ones.

Like Ryan. Lead singer of the band Rhiannon.

So hot it hurts, he can have any woman he wants. (And has, if the rumours are to be believed, and why wouldn't I believe them?)

But he keeps trying. And I don't understand it. He shows up at the Winter Wonderland. Sends me an MP3 player full of music to keep me company on a long drive.

So maybe I'll give in. At least, long enough to get it out of our systems. I mean, once he gets what he wants, he'll disappear, right?

Never mind how I'll feel when he does.

***Chasing Alys* is a slow burn steamy rockstar romance. It is the first book following Rhiannon and the first in the True Platinum Series. If you enjoy obsessed cinnamon roll heroes, take no-nonsense heroines and hook ups**

gone wrong, you'll love Chasing Alys.

Winning Nia - Book 2

I don't need a rockstar to be my knight in shining armour. Especially one who already had his chance.

My first love broke my heart when I was sixteen. James Tyler was everything I'd ever wanted, until he up and left. That's what I get for falling for a musician whose plans for world domination never included me.

My second love, photography, would never let me down.

Or so I thought until I discovered that making it as a music photographer is a lot harder in reality than in my dreams – and my savings account can only take a beating for so long before I have to swallow my pride and start grovelling to my arrogant, estranged father. And if things couldn't get any worse, James is back...

Arriving with a job offer I shouldn't refuse, and a confession big enough to send shockwaves through the past, he throws my entire life upside down. But I don't care how successful his band is or that he insists I'm the one for him. If he thinks I forgive him tossing me aside ten years ago, he's got another thing coming.

To anyone else, James is a second chance wrapped in muscle and black ink. Too bad for him, I've never believed in second chances.

Winning Nia is a full length steamy rock star romance. It is the second book following the Rhiannon men and the second in the True Platinum Series. Can be read as a standalone.

If you love obsessed rock stars, determined independent heroines who want to solve their own problems and childhood sweethearts getting a second chance, then Winning Nia is for you.

Enticing Mel - Book 3

What happens when your past catches up with your present? I'm not sure I want to know.

Five years ago, my childhood sweetheart left me with more than a broken heart as his band rose to stardom. I've tried to move on and build a life without him.

I should've known the peace wouldn't last. Eventually, his band would come home, and I'd be forced to face the dreamy bassist who still owns my heart. But I've been hiding something and my secret is about to be revealed.

As much as I don't want his flaky lifestyle impacting my daughter — our daughter — I can't lie anymore. Dan still makes my heart flutter and steals my breath.

He's sure we can pick up where we left off now that he's not touring. But I'm not the carefree girl anymore, and I'm not sure I can let him in again, not when someone else's heart is on the line.

Will I listen when my head says no? Or

will he be able to entice my heart once more?

Enticing Mel is a steamy rock star romance. It's the third book following the Rhiannon men and the third in the True Platinum Series. Can be read as a standalone.

If you love obsessed rock stars and childhood sweethearts getting a second chance with a secret baby keeping the heroine on her toes, then Enticing Mel is for you.

Defying Ella - book 4

One cabin, one badly timed snowstorm, and one asshole drummer. What could possibly go wrong?

He has it – that thing. You know the one I mean, right?
It's not just the natural-born talent that cascades from him in musical waves

when he's on stage, and it's more than drive, more than passion.

It's the one indescribable thing I can't nail down for myself, and the man I despise more than anything right now, is throwing it away like it's nothing. It's infuriating.

He's infuriating.

I didn't expect to spend so much time with him, near him, on this tour. And so, when the opportunity arose to escape to the quiet of the cabin, I took it. Only for the self-obsessed prick to turn up not long after.

Now, I can't escape him and the reminders of the week we shared, what feels like a lifetime ago.

He's got what I want, what I need. But can he help me find mine? And do I even want him to?

Defying Ella is a steamy rockstar romance. It is the fourth book following the Rhiannon men and the fourth in the True Platinum Series. Can be read as a standalone.

If you love bad boy rock stars with a secret soft side meeting their match in an optimistic, strong-willed heroine, then Defying Ella is for you.

Needing Emily - book 4.5

One night in Vegas with Owen Parry. It should have been simple. It wasn't.

He's hot. He's always been hot. Half of the problem is that he knows it - something the Marable following aren't shy about letting him know.
Of course, with a few drinks in hand, one thing led to another. You can see where this is going... What I wasn't expecting, was the ring I woke up wearing.
I'm not ashamed to say I ran. I have no doubt he's only looking for arm candy, this rock star life isn't made for marriage. For love.
Either way, the knock on my door

comes as a surprise. He's here, and he wants a chance to get to know his wife. Is there more to Owen than meets the eye, or should you always go with your gut?

Needing Emily is a steamy rock-star romance. It's an accompanying novella to the True Platinum Series. Can be read as a standalone.

If you love cinnamon roll rock stars that fight for what, and who, they want and a heroine struggling to believe she's enough, then Needing Emily is for you.

Braving Lily - Book 5

What happens when the limelight isn't all it was meant to be?

Lily

It's like the entire world is rushing

ahead and I just want to stop the ride, I want to get off.

I need a rest. A break. An easy half-hour with someone who doesn't have stars in their eyes and money on their mind.

So, I sold a date in a charity auction, and when the recipient doesn't even bother to turn up, I question whether normal men are worth the effort.

Turns out the rock star variety aren't. But it irks me. Men don't stand me up – nobody does. I'm Lily Tyler, goddamnit.

What I know of this man is enough to pique my interest, and I'm not going to take no for an answer now. I'm having this date, one way or another.

Rhys

A setup, with a rockstar, organised by my mother. That's not what I'm looking for.

Some self-entitled little girl looking for a doe-eyed boy to worship her, I think not.

It's safe to say, after my marriage

crumbled before my eyes, that I'm not interested in opening myself up to any kind of heartbreak again, ever.

But when I find myself backed into a corner, when she's asking for nothing more than a coffee, can I say no?

Will Lily manage to strong-arm her way into this date? Will Rhys get more than he bargained for if she does?

Braving Lily is a steamy rock star romance. It's the fifth book in the True Platinum series. Can be read as a standalone.

If you love strong and sassy rock stars falling for the heartbroken boy next door, then Braving Lily is for you.

Daring Ceri - Book 6

The spotlights stole her heart once. Now they're stealing her future — and she's not leaving without a fight.

Alex

Who knew a drunken ceremony in Fiji could be legally binding? Not me, but I'm not complaining.

I couldn't figure out how to make her give me a second chance, how to prove I've changed from the jerk who dumped her years ago. Now I have my chance to show her the man I've become — and this time, the finale will be just the start.

Ceri

I'm engaged. I've moved on. Yet destiny drops the man who broke my heart back into my life with no warning.

Now the rock god who ditched me for fame is blackmailing me into a three-month tour that will wreck everything I've worked for.

I know better. Some days, I hate him. But despite our history, his rhythm still calls to me.

I won't be another conquest. If he thinks I'll surrender to the same fantasy that ruined me before, he's wrong.

But refusing him could mean losing it all.

Daring Ceri is a steamy enemies-to-lovers rock star romance following two childhood sweethearts and an eight-year-old accidental marriage.

For readers who love forced proximity, second chance love, and the kind of romance that never fades.

Marrying Olivia - Book 7

A rockstar romance that began with "I do"...and led to the love of a lifetime.

Olivia

All I wanted was to share my music with the world. Then I woke up married to Lewis, the sexy bassist of the band I'm opening for. Our drunken Vegas wedding was a mistake. A lie. A joke that went too far...

I'm determined to annul our marriage. He lives for the fame and excess of the rockstar life. I live for my music and changing the world. We have nothing in common. And yet, the way his stormy eyes seem to see into my soul ignites a fire I can't ignore...

Lewis

I'm living every rockstar's dream. Money. Parties. Fans. Then I meet Olivia, the opening act with the voice of an angel, and end up married after a reckless night in Vegas—definitely not my usual style.

But Olivia sees something in me that makes me want to be better. I never plan to fall for a small town girl. But she's the only duet I want, and a love this big is worth fighting for.

If you love steamy rockstar romances, opposites attracting and love stories that begin with an "I do," this book is for you.

There will be at least three more books in the True Platinum series, including Marrying Olivia (2024 - Lewis), Craving Leah (2024 - Andy), and Resisting Aisling (2025 - Tom).

ALSO BY MORGANA BEVAN

True Platinum Series (Rock Star Romance)

(Rhiannon)

Chasing Alys – Ryan (Resistant to Love)

Charming Daphne – Matt (Force Proximity)

Winning Nia – James (Second Chance)

Enticing Mel – Dan (Secret Baby)

Needing Emily – Emily (Accidental Marriage/Runaway Bride)

Defying Ella - Jared (Close Proximity / Snowed-In)

(The Brightside)

Braving Lily - Lily (Opposites Attract)

Daring Ceri - Alex (Second Chance)

Kings of Screen Series (Hollywood Romance)

Between Takes (Enemies to Lovers)

Married Blind (Marriage of Convenience)

Acting Counsel (Close Proximity,
Forbidden)

Fashionably Fake (Fake Dating)

Sign up for Morgana Bevan's mailing list:
https://morganabevan.com/mailing-list/

Morgana Bevan is a sucker for a rock star romance, particularly if it involves a soul-destroying breakup or strangers waking up in Vegas. She's a contemporary romance author based in Wales. When Morgana's not writing steamy celebrity romances with gorgeous British rock stars and movie stars, she's travelling the world, searching for inspiration.

She enjoys travelling, attending gigs, and trying out the extreme activities she forces on her characters.

Find Morgana online at morganabevan.com.